8-12

THE MYSTERY OF LIFE ON OTHER PLANETS

REVISED AND UPDATED

Chris Oxlade

Heinemann Library

Chicago, Illinois

Customer Service 888-454-2279

Visit our website at www.heinemannraintree.com

Editorial: Adam Miller, Catherine Veitch
Design: Philippa Jenkins
Production: Vicki Fitzgerald
Originated by Chroma Graphics (Overseas) Pte. Ltd
Printed and bound in China by Leo Paper Group
12 11 10 09 08
10 9 8 7 6 5 4 3 2 1

New edition ISBNs: 978-1-4329-1020-4 (hardcover)
                   978-1-4329-1026-6 (paperback)

Library of Congress Cataloging-in-Publication Data
Oxlade, Chris.
  The mystery of life on other planets / Chris Oxlade.
    p. cm. -- (Can science solve?)
  Includes bibliographical references and index.
  Summary: Examines the question of life on other planets, and its scientific exploration in the space program and more.
   ISBN 1-58810-666-7
  1. Life on other planets--Juvenile literature
  [1. Life on other planets. 2. Outer space--Exploration.] I. Title. II. Series.
  QB54. O58 2002
  567.8'39--dc21
                        2001004539

Acknowledgments
The author and publisher are grateful to the following for permission to reproduce copyright material:
© Corbis: pp**19, 28**; © Fortean Picture Library: pp**7, 9, 27**; © NASA: pp**16, 18, 21**; © Rex Features: p**4**; © S. Lowry: p**12**; © Science Photo Library: pp**5, 6, 8, 11, 13, 14, 15, 17, 20, 22, 23, 25, 26, 29**.

Cover artwork of a moon above the surface of an extrasolar gas giant planet © Science Photo Library/ Detlev van Ravensway.

The publishers would like to thank Geza Gyuk and Charlotte Guillain for their assistance in the preparation of this book.

Every effort has been made to contact copyright holders of any material reproduced in this book. Any omissions will be rectified in subsequent printings if notice is given to the publishers.

Some words are shown in bold, **like this**. You can find the definition for these words in the glossary.

CONTENTS

UNSOLVED MYSTERIES

For centuries, people have been puzzled and fascinated by mysterious places, creatures, and events. Is there really a monster in Loch Ness? Did the lost city of Atlantis ever exist? Are crop circles messages from **aliens** or clever **hoaxes**? Are unidentified flying objects (UFOs) alien spacecraft, or simply tricks of the light? Is there alien life on Mars or Venus? Some of these mysteries have baffled scientists, who have spent years trying to find the answers. But just how far can science go? Can it really explain the unexplained? Are there some mysteries that science simply cannot solve? Read on and try to make up your own mind . . .

This book tells you about the search for alien life. It looks at eyewitness accounts of alien life, at the methods that **astronomers** and other scientists are using to try to find signs of **extraterrestrial** life, and at what successes they have had so far.

The creators of hundreds of movies and TV shows have tried to guess what aliens would look like.

Are we alone?

When you watch **science fiction** movies or television programs or read a science fiction book, do you ever wonder whether the aliens shown in them could really exist? You might ask similar questions when you look up at the night sky. Are there other animals and plants out there in space? Or is Earth the only place in the **universe** where life exists? In other words—are we alone?

Finding out about life on other planets is not just a matter of curiosity. It might help us to understand the universe and how it works, how life on Earth started in the first place, how the human race developed, and what might happen to it in the distant future.

On one hand, alien life seems very unlikely. Some scientists think that we might be the only intelligent life in our **galaxy**, or even in the universe. On the other hand, why should Earth be unique? Other scientists think that there simply must be other intelligent life in the universe.

This book looks at two main questions: Is there (or was there) life elsewhere in our **solar system**? Are there planets outside our solar system where life could exist?

Are there other planets like Earth among the billions of stars?

BEGINNINGS OF A MYSTERY

Nobody knows when people first started to wonder whether there is other life in the universe. Until a few hundred years ago, most people believed that Earth was at the center of the universe. They did not know what the stars were or about the other planets in the **solar system**, which they thought were "wandering" stars.

The invention of the telescope in the 17th century allowed **astronomers** to see that these wandering stars were actually solid planets that reflected light from the Sun, rather than making light themselves. One of the first scientists to say it was possible that life existed on other planets was the Dutch astronomer Christiaan Huygens (1629–1695). At the time, there was no reason to believe that it did not.

Martian "canals"

Only 100 years ago, many top scientists still thought it was perfectly possible that there was life on our neighboring planet, Mars. This was due largely to the Italian astronomer Giovanni Schiaparelli (1835–1910), who examined the surface of Mars through telescopes and described the long, straight channels he saw.

This is one of Percival Lowell's (see right) sketches of Martian canals.

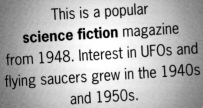

This is a popular **science fiction** magazine from 1948. Interest in UFOs and flying saucers grew in the 1940s and 1950s.

The Italian word for channels is "*canali*," which was wrongly translated as "canals."

Soon everybody was talking about Martians! Among them was the U.S. astronomer Percival Lowell (1855–1916). He spent years studying the "canals." He believed that they had been built by intelligent beings to carry water to dry areas of the planet and water crops there. When space probes finally visited Mars in the 1960s, they found no trace of these canals. They can only have been some sort of **optical illusion**.

The Guzman Prize

In Paris in 1900 a prize of 100,000 French francs (a huge amount of money at the time) was offered to the first person to communicate with **extraterrestrials**. Contact with Martians was excluded, because people were convinced that there was life on Mars, and that contacting them would be too easy!

SEEING THE ALIENS

The easiest way to solve our mystery would be to actually see aliens from other planets! So, has anybody ever seen alien life?

The only **extraterrestrial** place that people have visited is the Moon. The astronauts who landed there in the 1960s and 1970s did not see any signs of life, but most **astronomers** accepted that the Moon was a dead world long before this. The only other places we have seen are the surfaces of Mars, Venus, and Saturn's moon, Titan. These places have been photographed by space probes that have landed. Their cameras saw no life, either.

One sighting of a life-form that some scientists think might be alien is in the form of a fossil in a lump of rock. The rock is a **meteorite** that originated on Mars. The fossil could be of a tiny **microorganism**.

Several Apollo missions to the Moon by U.S. astronauts proved that it is a lifeless world.

Alien sightings on Earth

Every year people claim to have seen hundreds of UFOs in the sky. The vast majority of these are caused by the weather or are actually aircraft. But a few remain unexplained. Some people believe that these are alien spacecraft spying on us. Some people say they have met aliens on Earth, and some even claim that they have been whisked away by aliens for a few hours. No UFO report has ever been backed up by any physical evidence. Here are two typical eyewitness accounts of aliens.

U.S. military pilot Kenneth Arnold was the first person to use the phrase "flying saucer" to describe the UFO he saw in 1947.

Goose Bay, Labrador, Canada, 1954

Three hours into a flight from New York to London, the captain of a Stratocruiser airliner saw seven UFOs in a formation. The airliner's crew and several passengers described the UFOs as globes—six small and one large. The UFOs kept pace with the airliner for 20 minutes, occasionally changing formation, but when a military jet was sent to investigate them, they disappeared.

Kelly Hopkinsville, Kentucky, 1955

On a summer evening, Billy Ray Taylor was staying with friends on their farm and went out to get water from the well. He saw a UFO, which he described as very bright with a multicolored exhaust. His friends assumed he had seen a shooting star. But an hour later, several short creatures with glowing bodies and huge heads and ears approached the house. The owners shot at them, but the bullets did no harm. In the morning there was no trace of the creatures.

PLANETS, MOONS, AND STARS

Before we can think about whether alien life could exist in the universe, we need to understand a bit about the size and structure of the universe, and about how stars and planets like our Sun and Earth are formed.

Solar systems

Earth is one member of a family of planets that **orbit** the Sun, which is our local star. The Sun, the planets, and the moons that orbit the planets are known as the **solar system**. The solar system formed out of an enormous cloud of gas and dust. **Gravity** pulled the gas and dust together to form the Sun. Leftover material formed the planets and moons.

The life of a star

In the center of a star there are **nuclear reactions** happening that create huge amounts of **energy**. The star gives out this energy as heat, light, and other forms of **radiation**.

A solar system is a family of planets orbiting a star.

The Sun is a pretty average sort of star. It started shining about 4.6 billion years ago and will shine for another 5 billion years. Before it dies, it will expand, swallowing up the inner planets, possibly including Earth.

Unmanned spacecraft can visit planets in our solar system. This photograph of the surface of Mercury was taken by Mariner 10 in 1974.

Making Earth

Our solar system contains some small planets with rocky surfaces, such as Earth and Mars, and some large planets with a deep **atmosphere**, called the gas giants, such as Jupiter and Saturn. Earth formed about 4.6 billion years ago. It started life as a ball of molten rock. For 1 billion years, it was bombarded by lumps of rock floating around in space. It was also covered in volcanoes. The oceans formed about 4 billion years ago. The atmosphere formed even earlier, but it was not like the atmosphere we know. It did not contain the oxygen we need to breathe.

The size of the universe

All the stars you can see in the night sky are members of a huge group of stars called the Milky Way. The Milky Way is a **galaxy**. It contains hundreds of billions of stars, and is about 100,000 **light-years** across. (A light-year is the distance that light travels in a year—about 5.9 trillion miles or 9.5 trillion kilometers.) More staggering still is the fact that the universe contains many billions of galaxies! And many of the stars in these galaxies should have solar systems of their own.

WHAT IS LIFE?

What do you think of when you hear the word "life"? You probably think of humans and the thousands of other species of animals, trees, and flowers. But remember that most organisms on Earth are microorganisms, such as bacteria, that you can only see through a microscope. The easiest definition of life is an organism that grows and reproduces itself.

Conditions for life

Animals, plants, and other organisms must have certain things in order to grow and live. The most important requirements are water in liquid form (rather than ice or steam) and a source of energy. Animals get energy from the food they eat, and plants get energy from sunlight. Life likes warm, wet places best, as you can see from the abundant life in rainforests.

What makes a planet suitable for life?

Life can only exist on planets where conditions are suitable. This means that a planet must be close enough to its star for water to remain liquid, but not so close that it boils away. Astronomers call this region the "habitable zone." Earth is inside the habitable zone of the Sun. For life to exist on the surface, a planet must also have an atmosphere that cuts out harmful rays from the Sun.

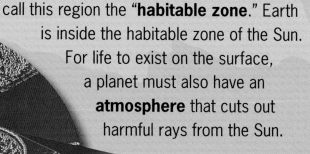

Bacteria can be found in all environments on Earth. Is it possible that these tiny organisms could be found on other planets?

Life in strange places

In recent years microorganisms have been found in some pretty nasty places. For example, green **algae** have been found living under rocks in dry, cold Arctic regions, inside rocks in dry, hot deserts, and in piping hot water next to **geysers**. Perhaps most amazingly, microorganisms have been found living next to thermal vents several miles under the sea. There is no light there, so the organisms get energy from the water, which is so hot that on the surface it would be boiling. Bacteria have been discovered miles deep within Earth. This means that the surface of a planet is only one place in which to look for life.

Microorganisms can also survive **dormant** for thousands of years, even in space. Apollo 12 astronauts found bacteria on a camera that had been left there two years earlier! These findings tell us that life can exist in places where scientists previously thought that it could not survive.

Some bacteria can even survive near volcanic vents, many miles below the surface of the oceans.

LIFE FROM SOUP

We know that Earth was formed around 4.6 billion years ago. It started its life as a huge ball of molten rock where life could not exist. And we know that now there are millions of different **species** of animals and plants that inhabit almost the whole surface of Earth, including intelligent life, such as humans, great apes, and dolphins. So where did life on Earth come from? What did the first forms of life look like? And how did we develop from them?

Why we need to know

If we can find out and understand how life began on Earth, and what the conditions on Earth were like when it started, we will be able to understand how life could start (or could have already started) on other planets, and look for planets where the conditions are the same today.

Scientists from several different branches of science are involved in trying to find out how and when life started on Earth. They include **geologists**, **climatologists**, **paleontologists**, and **biochemists**.

Paleontologists study the fossilized remains of animals and plants to try to understand how life evolved.

The theory so far

At the moment, we still do not actually know how life started, but there is a theory. Millions of years after Earth was formed, oceans began to form from water in the **atmosphere**. Huge electric storms raged all the time, and **meteorites** were crashing into the surface. Under these conditions, it is thought that simple chemicals reacted together to form more complex chemicals in the oceans.

The oceans full of chemicals are known as the primeval soup. Somehow, more than 3.5 billion years ago, these complex chemicals reacted together to form extremely simple **organisms** that could recreate themselves. The latest theory is that this happened near **hydrothermal vents** under the sea, quite by accident.

These organisms were our **ancestors**! Life remained very simple for another two billion years before simple plants such as **algae** developed, then more complex plants and simple animals. Over hundreds of millions of years, the different species we know today have **evolved**.

If it is true that life started **spontaneously** on Earth from a mixture of chemicals, then there is no reason to think that the same thing could not happen in similar conditions elsewhere in the **universe**.

This meteorite crater is in Arizona. The enormous **energy** of an impact could have caused chemical reactions in the primeval soup.

LIFE IN OUR SOLAR SYSTEM

The easiest place for us to look for **alien** life is in our own **solar system**. We can see the surfaces of other planets with powerful telescopes, but not well enough to see the details that would indicate life. However, we can investigate the conditions on other planets by examining them with special telescopes and by sending probes. This way we can get an idea of whether they could support life.

Even the chances of life on the Moon could not be ruled out until astronauts landed there in 1969. The astronauts went into quarantine when they arrived back on Earth, just in case they were carrying microscopic life back with them!

The Mars Reconnaissance Orbiter sends back data about the atmosphere and surface of Mars. This information gives scientists a better idea about whether Mars could ever have supported life.

Our habitable zone

Remember that **astronomers** call the region around a star where life could exist on planets the **habitable zone**. Mercury, Jupiter, Saturn, Uranus, and Neptune are outside the habitable zone of our Sun. Venus, Earth, and Mars are inside it. Venus has a thick **atmosphere** containing sulfuric acid, and the temperature on the surface is more than 840°F (450°C). So life on this planet is impossible. But it might have existed billions of years ago.

How do we know about planets?

Astronomers use special telescopes, such as infrared telescopes, to investigate the surfaces or atmospheres of the planets and their moons. They can find out what temperature the surface is and what chemicals are in the atmosphere. Space probes have **orbited** and landed on most of the planets and several moons. They have taken photographs, used **radar** to make maps, and measured the chemical composition of their atmospheres and surface rocks.

Is there life lurking under the icy surface of Jupiter's moon, Europa?

Life on Europa?

Although Jupiter is outside the habitable zone, the Galileo probe that flew close to its moon, Europa, in the mid-1990s seemed to show that there is an ocean of liquid water underneath its icy surface. Could conditions in the water be right for life?

LIFE ON MARS

Although our neighboring planet, Mars, is only half the size of Earth, it is similar to Earth in several ways. Its day is about the same length, it has a thin **atmosphere**, and it has polar **ice caps** that look like Earth's ice caps. Mars seems to be the most likely place to find **extraterrestrial** life in our **solar system**. On the next four pages you can find out how **astronomers** and other scientists are trying to find life there.

Probes to Mars

The first space probe to visit Mars was Mariner 4 in 1965. It took photographs of a small section of the planet's surface. To the dismay of the **NASA** mission scientists, the photographs showed a cratered surface like the surface of the Moon, with no signs of life. Two more probes in 1969 showed the same features in different places.

This photograph of the surface of Mars was taken by NASA's Mars Rover.

In 1971 another probe, Mariner 9, arrived to map the whole surface of Mars. Scientists were amazed to see pictures of huge volcanoes, including one 16 miles (25 kilometers) high, and deep chasms, like dry riverbeds, hundreds of miles wide. The scientists concluded that these chasms must have been eroded by vast quantities of flowing water, and so they immediately thought of the possibility of life. They planned a mission to land on the surface and test for life.

Viking tests for life

The Viking probes landed on Mars in 1976. They collected Martian soil with a scoop and carried out experiments to test for **microorganisms**. In two experiments, a sample of soil was dropped into a liquid containing food. If there were microorganisms in the soil, they would digest the food, making waste gases such as oxygen and carbon dioxide in the process. The two experiments tested for these gases. A third experiment tested for **photosynthesis**, which would show that there were simple plants, such as **algae**, in the soil.

A Viking lander scoops up Martian soil to test it for simple life.

NASA scientists were delighted and amazed when all three of these experiments gave positive results. But then the results of another experiment showed that there were no **organic chemicals** in the soil, which meant that life could not exist there. The scientists realized that the positive tests were the result of other chemicals in the Martian soil. For the time being, hope for life on Mars was shattered.

FRESH HOPE FOR MARTIAN LIFE

Today, there is fresh hope of finding life on Mars. There are several reasons for this. The discovery of green **algae** living inside rocks in very cold, very dry Arctic regions of Earth suggests that **microorganisms** could live in the sort of conditions found on the surface of Mars, although the conditions on Mars are far more severe. Future probes to Mars will look inside rocks. Rocks might also contain fossils of **organisms** that lived on Mars millions of years ago, when conditions were more like those on Earth. The Mars Exploration Rovers, Spirit and Opportunity, landed on Mars in 2004. They have already produced evidence that some parts of Mars had substantial amounts of liquid water in the past.

The Martian meteorite

In 1996 hope for life on Mars was given a boost by the discovery of what may be a fossil of a Martian microorganism. It was found inside a **meteorite** called ALH84001, which was discovered in Antarctica in 1984.

Are these tube-like structures fossilized remains of microorganisms? Scientists believe that the meteorite they were found in may have come from Mars.

This image from the **NASA** Orbiter shows the effects of ancient underground fluids on Mars.

Experts think the meteorite came from Mars because it contained little pockets of gas that matched the gas in the Martian **atmosphere**. They think it was formed when a monster meteor hit Mars, throwing rock out into space.

Inside the meteorite are what look like fossils of microorganisms. They resemble tiny worms. The discovery caused a sensation around the world. Evidence of life on Mars had finally been found! Or had it? Investigations cannot show if it is actually is a fossil, so there is no proof. The subject is still being debated.

Did we arrive by accident?

The fact that meteorite ALH84001 and several other meteorites were discovered to have come from Mars shows that pieces of one planet can end up falling on another, even though the planets are millions of miles apart. Some scientists think it is possible that life on Earth did not start on its own, but rather was brought from Mars on a meteorite. So we may all be descended from Martian microorganisms!

21

THE SEARCH FOR OTHER PLANETS

We have looked at the possibility of life on other planets in our **solar system**, but what about planets outside it? We know that there are countless billions of stars in the **universe**, many of them similar to our Sun. It seems likely that there should be planets (called **extrasolar planets**) **orbiting** these stars, too. The first step in the search for life outside the solar system is to find other Earth-like planets.

Too small to see

The problem with finding extrasolar planets is that they are so far away! The nearest star to the Sun is four **light-years** away. At that distance, spotting an Earth-sized planet is like spotting a tennis ball on the Moon! Another problem is that any light reflected from a planet would be swamped by the light from its star.

The Hubble Space Telescope has taken photographs that seem to show planets around distant stars.

Spot the wobble

At the moment, the only way to tell whether there are planets orbiting another star is to use powerful telescopes to look for the effects that planets have on a star. There are two main effects. The first is that as planets orbit a star, their **gravity** makes the star wobble very slightly back and forth. We can just spot these wobbles from Earth, but only if the planets are very big. The second effect is that as a planet passes between the star and Earth, it blocks out a tiny bit of the light from the star. This makes the star twinkle very slightly.

Planets as close to their stars as Mercury would probably be far too hot to support life.

The search continues

The first proof of a planet outside the solar system came in 1995. Since then, **astronomers** have found evidence of around 250 extrasolar planets. For example, a planet half the size of Jupiter is orbiting a star called 51 Pegasi, which is 50 light-years from Earth. A planet about the same size as Jupiter is orbiting a star 50 light-years away, called 47 Ursae Majoris, in the Big Dipper.

The problem is that many of these planets are closer to their stars than Mercury is to our Sun, showing that their solar systems are very different from our own and are unlikely to have Earth-like planets. But the search for rocky planets like Earth continues. There are plans to develop a scientific instrument, called the Terrestrial Planet Finder, that would go into space to look for them.

WAITING FOR SIGNALS

Even if we do detect Earth-like planets in other solar systems, how can we prove that there is life on them? Using current space technology, sending probes would be impractical. They would take a hundred thousand years to reach even our nearest star.

Signals from other planets

Some scientists think that the best way to look for life outside the solar system is to look for signs of advanced technology. This assumes that intelligent life has evolved on other planets, and that it has developed technology at least as advanced as ours. There might, for example, be radio signals coming from other planets. These could have been sent deliberately by other intelligent life searching for us or could simply be signals that have escaped into space, in the same way that signals from our communications systems are going into space all the time. Because these signals travel at the speed of light, they would take only a few years to arrive on Earth.

The search is on

The first attempt to detect signals from other worlds was called project Ozma. The Ozma scientists aimed a **radio telescope** at two nearby stars similar to the Sun. They listened for 200 hours but found no signals.

The current search is called the Search for **Extraterrestrial** Intelligence (SETI). The SETI Institute was formed in 1984. It was originally paid for by **NASA**, but is now privately financed. Its Project Phoenix is searching for signals from **alien** life, using several huge radio telescopes around the world. They try to find radio signals coming from space that seem to have some sort of message in them. The telescopes are being aimed at stars within 200 **light-years** of Earth, where we know there is a chance of Earth-like planets being found.

Unfortunately, the telescopes also pick up messages that have come from communication systems on Earth. SETI uses two telescopes at once to try to filter out these confusing messages. Then computers search through any signals to try to find meaningful messages. So far no extraterrestrial signals have been detected.

An array of radio telescopes can detect extremely weak signals from space.

FAKES AND FRIGHTS

It would be very difficult to go to another planet, make some fake **alien** life, and have it discovered by scientists! So it is no surprise that nobody has ever claimed to have found aliens on another planet. However, plenty of people have faked photographs of alien spacecraft and creatures on Earth.

George Adamski, 1952

One of the most famous alien encounters involved 61-year-old George Adamski. It was the first report of a human meeting an alien. Adamski claimed that he had gone into the Californian desert to watch for UFOs. He had seen one—a cigar-shaped flying saucer— and close by was a figure, which he described as human-like, of average height, with tanned skin, long gold hair, and green eyes. Adamski talked to the alien in sign language and by **telepathy**, and he discovered that it came from Venus.

Later, Adamski claimed that he had met more aliens, and that they had taken him to meet other aliens on Venus, Mars, and other planets. At the time many people believed Adamski, but we now know that there is no life on the planets he mentioned. It is likely that he made everything up.

This is a reconstruction of an alien supposedly found at Roswell, New Mexico. Many people believe that aliens have visited Earth, but we can never be sure.

Why make fakes?

Why do people like Adamski try to fake sightings of spacecraft and aliens? One obvious reason is to try to make money by selling the story to a newspaper or by writing a book. In fact, Adamski published several best-selling books about aliens, including one called *Flying Saucers Have Landed.* Other people fake UFO photographs just for fun or to impress their friends.

Fact or fiction?

The report of visiting aliens that had the most effect on people was not a fake, but fiction. In 1898 H. G. Wells published a novel about a Martian invasion of Earth called *War of the Worlds.* Orson Welles made *War of the Worlds* into a radio play that was broadcast in the United States in 1938. An actor played the part of a radio reporter who watched the Martians as they attacked Earth in their tripod spacecraft, killing people with heat rays. The first episode caused panic among millions of radio listeners, who thought the reports were real! They called family and friends to tell them to leave New York, where the Martians were supposed to be heading.

WHAT DO YOU THINK?

So, can science really solve the mystery of life on other planets? To prove that **alien life existed**, scientists would need hard evidence, such as film of an alien or living bacteria from another planet. At the moment, we have no proof of the existence of alien life, either inside our solar system or on planets in other solar systems.

Will scientific advances give us the answer?

- We have found that there is water and there are other chemicals needed for life on other planets and moons in the solar system

- We have possibly discovered a fossil of an ancient Martian life-form

- We have found that there are hundreds of planets around other stars in our **galaxy**

- Scientists expect to find Earth-like planets outside our solar system in the next two decades. They think it will take around 100 years to find out if there is life on them.

BUT . . .
- There may be no alien life at all, in which case we will be looking forever!

Are there creatures on other planets exploring the space around them like we are?

Look at the accounts of alien sightings on page 9 and page 26 and think about the evidence in each case. Decide which accounts you think are the most convincing.

- Do you think that any of them might be true?

- Do you believe any of these witnesses, even though there has never been any physical evidence?

- Do you think that there must be other planets like Earth in the vastness of the **universe**, with animals and plants living on them?

- Or do you think that the chances of life starting elsewhere are just too small?

Now that you have read about the scientific investigations into **extraterrestrial** life, can you draw any conclusions? Try to keep an open mind. Bear in mind that if scientists throughout history had not bothered to investigate things that appeared to be strange or mysterious, many scientific discoveries may never have been made.

GLOSSARY

algae group of plants that lives in water and damp places. Some algae are made up of single plant cells.

alien living creature that does not come from Earth

ancestor person whom another person is descended from, or an animal that humans have evolved from

astronomer person who studies space and the objects in space

atmosphere blanket of gases around a planet. Only some planets have an atmosphere.

bacteria microscopically small organisms that are made up of a single cell. They are not animals or plants.

biochemist person who studies biochemistry, which is the science of the chemistry that happens inside living things

climatologist person who studies the world's climates and how they change

dormant not active at the moment

energy power or ability of something to make something else work, such as electricity and heat

evolve gradually develop new species over millions of years

extrasolar outside the solar system

extraterrestrial describes any object or being that does not come from Earth

galaxy huge group of stars in space. Galaxies can contain billions of stars. Our own galaxy is called the Milky Way.

geologist person who studies Earth, its history, and the rocks that make up Earth

geyser hole in the ground from which hot water and steam, heated by hot rocks underground, regularly shoot upward

gravity force that pulls things down

habitable zone area around a star where the conditions for life can exist on planets

hoax type of trick, where people say something has happened but it is not true

hydrothermal vent hole on the seabed, thousands of feet below the surface, from which hot, mineral-rich water escapes

ice cap thick covering of ice at the north or south pole of a planet

light-year distance light travels in a year, equivalent to 5.9 trillion miles (9.5 trillion kilometers)

meteorite piece of rock from space that hurtles through Earth's atmosphere and hits the ground, making a crater

microorganism organism that is too small to see with the naked eye, such as a bacterium

microscope device that makes a very small object look much larger. There are optical microscopes and electron microscopes.

NASA National Aeronautics and Space Administration in the United States

nuclear reaction splitting of the nucleus of an atom, or the joining together of two nuclei of two atoms

optical illusion image seen by the eye that is not what it seems. For example, a flip book shows a series of still pictures that appear animated.

orbit path that an object, such as a moon or a satellite, takes as it moves around a star or a planet

organic chemical chemical that is found in, or comes from, living things

organism anything that is living

paleontologist person who studies paleontology, which is the science of fossils

photosynthesis process by which plants make food using the energy in sunlight

radar device that can detect objects in the air. It sends out radio waves and detects any that bounce off objects and return. The objects are shown on the radar's screen.

radiation waves, rays, or streams of particles

radio telescope instrument that detects radio waves coming from objects in space. It has a dish-shaped antenna that collects the radio waves.

science fiction fictional stories about space or the future

solar system Sun and its family of planets and moons, or a similar group that centers around another star

spontaneously without outside influence

species group of animals or plants whose members share most features.

telepathy sensing what people are thinking by using extrasensory perception

universe everything that exists

Find out more

You can find out more about the search for life on other planets in books and on the Internet. Use a search engine such as www.yahooligans.com to search for information. Search for the words such as "life other planets" or "alien encounters."

More books to read

Herbst, Judith. *Aliens*.
Minneapolis: Lerner, 2005.
Royston, Angela. *Alien Neighbors?*
Chicago: Raintree, 2006.

Websites

www.nasa.gov Official site of NASA. Contains lots of information on NASA's Mars Exploration Program (mars.jpl.nasa.gov).
http://setiathome.berkeley.edu The SETI@home project is a scientific experiment that uses Internet-connected computers in the search for extraterrestrial intelligence. You can run a free program that downloads and analyzes radio telescope data.

INDEX